E
MO   Moncure, Jane Belk

          Word Bird's spring
          words

DATE			
AG 14 '87	MY 2 3 '89	JE 28 '90	MY 2 9 '92
SE 3 0 '87	JE 24 '89	JY 2 8 '90	JY 2 '92
OC 24 '87	JE 2 8 '89	OC 11 '90	JY 2 0 '92
MY 2 5 '88	JY 3 '89	AP 15 '91	AG 1 3 '92
JE 2 9 '88	JY 25 '89	JE 24 91	AP 1 9 '93
AG 2 0 '88	AG 9 '89	JY 2 2 '91	JAN 3
SE 15 '88	SE 1 4 '89	AG 2 2 '91	APR 94
DE 2 9 '88	FE 2 '90	OC 5 '91	JUL 14 '94
FE 2 9 '89	MR 3 '90	OC 15 91	JUN 2 4 '95
AP 1 7 '89	JR 2 3 '90	NO 1 '91	FEB 0 9 95
MY 1 '89	JE 1 2 '90	MR 3 1 '92	APR 1 0 95
			JUL 1 1 95

WORD BIRD'S SPRING WORDS

by Jane Belk Moncure
illustrated by Vera Gohman

THE
CHILD'S
WORLD

ELGIN, ILLINOIS 60120

Distributed by Childrens Press, 1224 West Van Buren Street, Chicago, Illinois 60607.

Library of Congress Cataloging in Publication Data

Moncure, Jane Belk.
  Word Bird's spring words.

  (Word house words for early birds)
  Summary: Word Bird puts words about spring in his word house—mud puddles, shamrocks, seeds, kites, and others.
  1. Vocabulary—Juvenile literature. 2. Spring—Juvenile literature. [1. Vocabulary. 2. Spring]
I. Gohman, Vera Kennedy, 1922-   ill. II. Title.
III. Series: Moncure, Jane Belk.   Word house words for early birds.
PE1449.M53 1985   428.1   85-5902
ISBN 0-89565-310-9

2 3 4 5 6 7 8 9 10 11 12 R 91 90 89 88 87 86

WORD BIRD'S
SPRING WORDS

Word Bird made a …

word house.

"I will put spring words
in my house," he said.

He put in these words –

rain

raincoat

boots

umbrella

mud puddles

tadpoles

frogs

leprechaun

shamrocks

hoe

seeds

water hose

garden

wind

kites

ball

bat

skates

robins

Easter eggs

Easter bunny

Easter basket

daffodils

May baskets

Can you read these spring word

rain

leprechaun

raincoat

shamrocks

boots

hoe

umbrella

seeds

mud puddles

water hose

tadpoles

frogs

garden

with 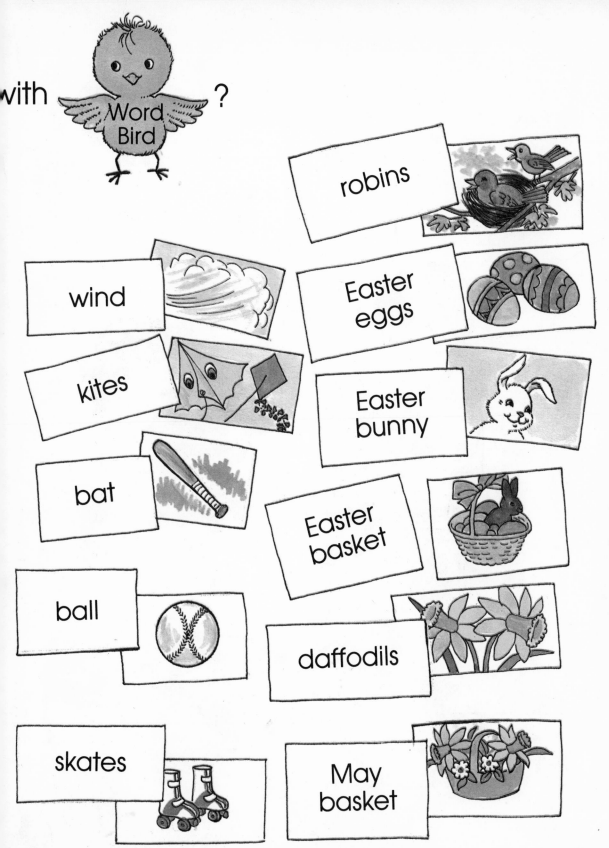 Word Bird?

robins

wind

Easter eggs

kites

Easter bunny

bat

Easter basket

ball

daffodils

skates

May basket

You can make a spring word house. You can put Word Bird's words in your house and read them too.